TRACTOR TOM'S
SPORTS
DAY

by Rebecca Gee

First published 2003 by Contender Books
Contender Books is a division of
The Contender Entertainment Group
48 Margaret Street
London W1W 8SE
www.contendergroup.com/books

**For more Tractor Tom fun and games, log on to his website
http://www.tractortom.com**

This edition published 2003
1 3 5 7 9 10 8 6 4 2

Tractor Tom™ © Contender Ltd 2002
Text © Contender Ltd 2003

Great Ormond Street Hospital Children's Charity.
Registered charity no. 235825.
The Contender Entertainment Group will give 5p from the sale of this
Tractor Tom product to Great Ormond Street Hospital Children's Charity.

ISBN 1 84357 087 4

Text by Rebecca Gee
Designed by BURVILLE RILEY
Production by Kate Gribble
Printed in Hong Kong by Printing Express Ltd.

THIS BOOK BELONGS TO
TRACTOR TOM'S FRIEND

....

It is a very special day on Springhill Farm. The postman has brought a surprise parcel for Tractor Tom. Fi goes outside to open it.

'It's a new mower to help Tom cut the grass!' says Fi.

It is a special day for Matt, too. He is getting ready for the sports day in Beckton. He wants to win his race, so he's doing lots of exercises to make sure he's really fit.

Tom loves his new mower. It is really fast.

'Well done, Tom!' says Fi. 'We'll cut the grass in this field in no time!'

Just then, Matt jogs past Tom and Fi's field.

'Hello Matt!' calls Fi, 'What are you doing?'

'I'm doing some last minute practice for the Beckton Sports Day,' cries Matt. 'I want to be ready to beat everyone in my race – and it's nearly time to go!'

Matt is just about to leave with Rev for the Beckton Sports Day when his mobile phone rings.

'Oh no!' Matt tells Rev, 'The ground in Beckton is flooded – they can't have a sports day after all!'

Matt is so disappointed, he goes to tell Fi and Tom.

Matt tells Fi and Tom all about the flood.

Tom knows just what to do to cheer him up! 'Tom-tom, tom-tom!' he tells Fi.

'Tom thinks we should have our own sports day right here in our newly mown field!' says Fi. 'What a great idea!'

Everyone gets ready for the first race. Wheezy, Purdey and Winnie wait nervously for the start.

'Ready… steady… go!' Fi shouts. Wheezy rumbles into life and heads for the finishing line. But Winnie's eating the grass and Purdey's still sleeping, so Wheezy wins easily!

'Congratulations Wheezy!' everyone cries.

Next it's time for the egg and spoon race!

'Come on, Fi, it's your turn now,' says Matt.

'On your marks… get set… go!' He shouts. They're off!

Fi, Riff and Snicker run as fast as they can… oops! Riff has dropped her egg and is out of the race!

Snicker gallops even harder and just beats Fi to the finish line. Well done Snicker!

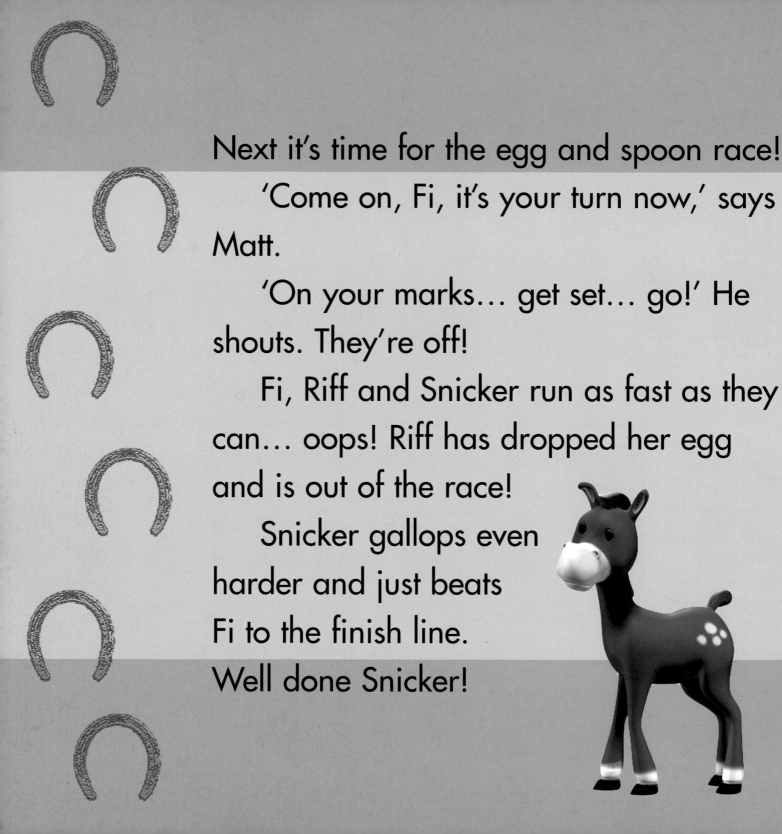

The last race of the day is the six-legged race for the sheep!

'Ready… steady… go!' Fi shouts, for the very last time.

The sheep soon tumble over each other and end up riding on each other's backs.

They get the loudest cheer of the day as they finish… all at the same time!

Fi and Matt share a special sports day cup – a nice cup of tea!

'Thank you for organising the best sports day ever, Fi,' says Matt.

'Don't thank me,' Fi smiles, 'Thank Tom. He cut the grass so quickly, we had somewhere to hold our own sports day.'

'Tom – what would we do without you?' cheers Matt.

IF YOU'VE ENJOYED THIS BOOK, CHECK OUT THESE OTHER TRACTOR TOM GOODIES - AVAILABLE NOW!

TRACTOR TOM AND THE MOBILE PHONE

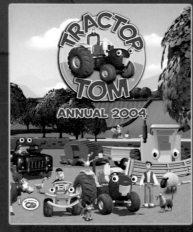

TRACTOR TOM ANNUAL 2004

TRACTOR TOM'S "WHERE'S IT GONE?" STICKER BOOK

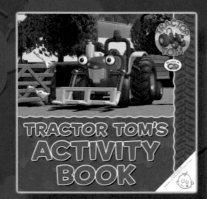

TRACTOR TOM'S ACTIVITY BOOK

No.1 FREE FARM ANIMALS AND PLAYMAT! IT'S MY FIRST ISSUE!

STORIES COLOURING PUZZLES

WHAT WOULD WE DO WITHOUT YOU?

BOOKS!

CLOTHES!

COMICS!

TOYS!

VIDEOS AND DVDS!

FOR MORE INFORMATION, PLEASE VISIT WWW.TRACTORTOM.COM

ViViD imaginations